# Courage to Fly

Story by Troon Harrison

Illustrated by Zhong-Yang Huang

Red Deer Press

Meg's family were island people who crossed the sea and came to the city.

Meg huddled small inside herself like a frightened bird. Apartment towers were dark fingers blocking the sun. Long shadows lay across the afternoon street when Meg came home from school. Her feet hurried past roaring gratings. Sirens wailed. Strangers jostled her.

The only place Meg felt safe was in her room, high above the street's commotion. Through the window, she watched swallows soar in a sky as blue as poster paint. She pressed her face sadly against the glass, watching children swoop below on skateboards and bicycles. They looked as free as the swallows. In Meg's room, the only sound was the rustle of pages turning. An empty feeling filled Meg's chest.

Sometimes Jenny, who lived down the hall, knocked on the apartment door.

"Can you come out to play?" Jenny asked. But Meg always shook her head no. She felt too small to brave the outdoors. Soon, Jenny stopped coming to knock.

One afternoon, some boys from Meg's class trailed her home. "Hey, Nutmeg!" they called. "Hey, nutty Meg!" They collected chestnuts and bounced them along the sidewalk at Meg's feet. She shrank even smaller inside herself and scuttled home.

In the courtyard by her apartment building, an old man was gliding through his set of exercises. The boys ran off, but Meg stopped to watch. The man's face creased into a smile.

"This is a move called Lonely Goose Leaves Flock," he said, and Meg nodded. She knew how that goose felt. "And this move is Wild Horse Chases Wind," he told her. Meg remembered how her legs used to gallop through happier days.

The old man stretched slowly and gracefully, looking loose and free. "This is Lying Tiger Listens to Wind," he said. Although the city roared all around him, the old man's face was peaceful and calm. "This is Gentle Wind Sweeps Leaves," he said.

Fallen leaves scattered across the pavement to drift at Meg's feet. She noticed their beautiful colors for the first time and gathered a handful to decorate her room.

Before the trees were bare, a sudden storm cloaked the city. Shrieking
children packed the snow into balls outside the school. One ball splattered
on Meg's back. She shrank beneath her collar and headed alone towards
home before anyone else noticed her. In the park, snowflakes iced golden
leaves. Meg squatted to take a closer look at something lying in the blue
shadows, beneath the iron railing.

The swallow was motionless. Its eyes were closed, its wings folded. Snow dusted its feathers and beak. Gently, Meg curled her mitts around the bird. Then she hurried home, not looking back when Jenny called her name. She rushed into the kitchen.

"Is it dead?" she asked.

Her mother stroked the blue feathers. "No, but it be very cold," she replied. "Maybe we put it in a box."

From a closet, Meg pulled out a cardboard box. She folded newspaper to cover the bottom. She ran water into a plastic container and spooned the baby's pureed beef into a metal lid. Then her mother laid the swallow in the box. Meg longed for the bird to open its eyes and find itself in a safe place.

In the morning, the swallow was upright in a corner of the box. Meg noticed how its wings swept to a point, how light gleamed on its head and in its bright eyes. "Don't worry, little bird," she crooned. "I'll keep you safe."

It was Saturday, so there was no school. Meg propped a book on her knee and waited for the swallow's twittering song — but it remained silent.

"That snow come down so early, it surprise this pretty bird," said Meg's mother after lunch. "It need to fly away south. It need to go where the sun be warm."

"I'm not letting it go," said Meg stubbornly. "I'll keep it safe until spring."

Melting snow dripped against Meg's window, but the swallow in the box was silent and still. The old man began his exercises again in the courtyard below. Meg dragged on her coat. She folded the flaps of the box shut and carried it carefully down the stairs.

Patiently she waited while the old man turned and balanced,
flowing through the movements.

"Can a swallow live in a box?" she asked at last.

His gentle eyes seemed to look right into her heart. "Watch," he said. "This move is called Swallow Skims Water . . . and this one is Swallow Penetrates Clouds. There are no clouds and no lakes inside a box."

"But outside — maybe it will die," said Meg.

"Ah, maybe," the old man agreed. "But in a box, it will die for certain. You have to give the swallow its chance. It has the courage it needs to fly."

Meg thought of the chestnut trees and gangs of boys in the park. She thought of the big dogs that loped over the grass. Then she thought about her safe, quiet room. The old man was watching her.

Jenny skipped around the corner of the apartment building, and Meg clutched her box tighter. "Can you come to the park with me?" she whispered shyly.

Jenny looked surprised.

"Sure," she agreed.

The old man smiled.

"This move is called Part Clouds and See Sun," he told them, his arms reaching for the sky.

"You come too," Meg invited.

"My old legs will follow," he said.

The girls splashed across the courtyard. Light shimmered beneath their boots.

In the park, the sun stretched bright fingers between the trees, touching the wet grass.

Meg opened the box and lifted the swallow out while Jenny watched. For one moment it clutched her fingers with tiny feet. Then it skimmed over the pond and arrowed upward. Meg tilted her face, watching the bird heading south toward warm air, its sleek wings tipped with sun, a twittering song held in its throat. Its joy bubbled in her chest.

When the bird was a speck, Meg turned to Jenny. She tried out a smile and Jenny smiled back with the sun in her eyes.

"Can you stay and play?" Jenny asked.

"I have to go back — " Meg started to say. Then she took a deep breath. "Yes!" she said suddenly. "Yes, I can play!"

"Race you to the swings!" Jenny shouted.

Meg squashed the swallow's box flat so it would fit into the trash can. Then she chased after Jenny through the wet leaves. They began to laugh as they swooped over the treetops on the swings' creaking chains.

Beneath the trees, the old man smiled once more. "This move is called Wild Geese Flying In Pairs," he murmured, his arms as light and flexible as wings.

Northern Lights Books for Children are published by
Red Deer Press
813 MacKimmie Library Tower
2500 University Drive N.W.
Calgary Alberta Canada T2N 1N4
www.reddeerpress.com

**Credits**
Edited for the Press by Peter Carver
Cover and text design by Blair Kerrigan/Glyphics
Printed and bound in Canada for Red Deer Press

**Author's Acknowledgement**
With thanks to my partner, Chris Adamson, whose gracious sharing of Lok Hup made this story possible.

**Publisher's Acknowledgments**
Financial support provided by the Canada Council, the Department of Canadian Heritage, the Alberta Foundation for the Arts, a beneficiary of the Lottery Fund of the Government of Alberta, and the University of Calgary.

COMMITTED TO THE DEVELOPMENT OF CULTURE AND THE ARTS

**National Library of Canada Cataloguing in Publication Data**
Harrison, Troon, 1958–
Courage to fly
ISBN 0-88995-273-6
I. Huang, Zhong-Yang, 1949–  II. Title.
PS8565.A6587C68 2002       jC813'.54
C2002-910851-9
PZ7.H25616Co 2002

5  4  3  2  1

*Anna and Peter, may you each find your wings and blue sky.*
— Troon Harrison

*For my dear nieces Jean and Enid.*
— Zhong-Yang Huang

**Author's Note**
Lok Hup is a Taoist internal martial art. The set consists of sixty-six individually named moves.